Dirty Bertie

For Billy and Bernard, woof! ~ D R
For Seb and Isabelle with love from
Eric the cat ~ A M

STRIPES PUBLISHING LIMITED
An imprint of the Little Tiger Group
1 Coda Studios, 189 Munster Road,
London SW6 6AW

Imported into the EEA by Penguin Random House Ireland,
Morrison Chambers, 32 Nassau Street, Dublin D02 YH68

A paperback original
First published in Great Britain in 2022

Characters created by David Roberts
Text copyright © Alan MacDonald, 2022
Illustrations copyright © David Roberts, 2022

ISBN: 978-1-78895-390-0

FSC
www.fsc.org
MIX
Paper from
responsible sources
FSC® C171272

The Forest Stewardship Council® (FSC®) is a global, not-for-profit organization dedicated
to the promotion of responsible forest management worldwide. FSC® defines standards
based on agreed principles for responsible forest stewardship that are supported by
environmental, social, and economic stakeholders. To learn more, visit www.fsc.org

10 9 8 7 6 5 4 3 2

Dirty Bertie

POOP!

DAVID ROBERTS WRITTEN BY **ALAN MACDONALD**

LiTTLE TiGER
LONDON

Dirty Bertie

Collect all the Dirty Bertie books!

Worms!

Fleas!

Pants!

Burp!

Yuck!

Crackers!

Bogeys!

Mud!

Germs!

Loo!

Fetch!

Fangs!

Kiss!

Ouch!

Snow!

Pong!

Pirate!

Scream!

Toothy!

Dinosaur!

Zombie!

Smash!

Rats!

Horror!

Jackpot!

Aliens!

Fame!

Monster!

Disco!

Mascot!

Spider!

Trouble!

Bees!

Contents

1 Poop! 7

2 Teacher! 37

3 Extras! 67

POOP!

CHAPTER 1

Bertie liked going to the local park after
school. It had a playground, gardens
and bags of open space. It was the
perfect place for a kick about with
his friends while Whiffer zoomed off
chasing squirrels. Today though the park
was different. There were large signs
everywhere…

NO LITTER! NO CYCLING!
NO DOG FOULING!!

"What's going on?" asked Bertie. Eugene and Darren looked baffled.

Mr Monk, the grumpy head gardener, came marching towards them.

"You've read the signs then?" he said. "The Council wants the park kept safe and clean so I've introduced some new rules."

"Dog fouling?" said Bertie. "Dogs can't play football."

"Very funny," said Mr Monk. "It means no dog mess. From now on any dog I catch doing their business will be banned."

Banned? Bertie couldn't believe his

ears. If dogs couldn't poop in the park where could they poop?

"But I always clear up after Whiffer," he argued.

Mr Monk shook his head. "Makes no difference, rules are rules," he said. "No poop in this park – you've been warned."

NO LITTE
NO CYCLI
NO DO
FOULIN

Bertie watched him stomp off back
to his wheelbarrow. He thought the day
couldn't get much worse, but someone
else had arrived – Know-All Nick, and
he was carrying a poodle in
his arms.

"Since when did you
have a dog?" asked
Darren.

"I got her last week,
actually," boasted Nick,
setting her down. "This is
Flossy, isn't she the cleverest
dog in the world?"
Bertie thought Nick and Flossy
seemed strangely alike – both had the
same snooty expression and looked
way too pleased with themselves.
And Flossy's coat made her look like a

walking pom-pom. Whiffer padded over
to sniff her but Flossy ignored him.

"She better not poop in the park,"
said Darren. "Did you see the signs?"

"Oh they don't worry me, she's very
well trained," bragged Nick. "In fact she
only does her you-know-what when I
tell her."

Dirty Bertie

Bertie was amazed – a dog that pooped to order, after only one week? He still couldn't get Whiffer to lie down after two years!

"Anyway, we can't stop, Flossy needs her exercise," said Nick. "And I don't want her catching fleas from your smelly old mutt."

Bertie glared after him.

"Trust Nick to have a poodle," he said. "I bet she's never got muddy in her life."

Whiffer was tugging at his lead so Bertie set him free.

"Is that a good idea?" asked Eugene.

"It's fine, he never goes far," said Bertie.

"Come on," said Darren, "I thought we were playing football. You're in goal, Bertie."

"Me? I was goalie last time," argued Bertie. "What about Eugene?"

But Eugene was looking across the park to the trees.

"Can you see Whiffer?" he asked.

Bertie scanned the park for any sign of him. Maybe he shouldn't have let him off the lead after all?

Just then they heard a howl of rage.

"GARRRRRRRGH!"

It was Mr Monk. He was standing close to the path. His face had turned crimson and he was pointing to something on the grass. Bertie's heart sank as Whiffer trotted into view. He wagged his tail at the head gardener as if expecting a pat on the head.

"YOU!" Mr Monk bellowed at Bertie. *"OVER HERE! NOW!"*

Dirty Bertie

Bertie trailed over with a sigh. Mr Monk looked like he was about to explode. He pointed to a small, pongy pile on the grass.

"What do you call this?" he demanded.

Bertie inspected it. "It looks like dog poo," he said. Quite honestly he was surprised Mr Monk needed to ask.

CHAPTER 2

"Your dog did this," said Mr Monk.

"How do you know?" asked Bertie, putting Whiffer on his lead. "Any dog could have done it!"

"Rubbish!" snapped Mr Monk. "Do you see any other dogs around?"

Bertie looked about. There were two or three other dogs in the park, but they were all miles away with their owners. Nick and his snooty poodle were nowhere to be seen.

"I still say it wasn't Whiffer," Bertie protested. "You can't prove it."

"I don't need to," said Mr Monk. "You saw the signs, I gave you fair warning. That's it – your dog's banned from the park."

"What?" gasped Bertie.

"You can't do that!" cried Darren.

"Just watch me," said Mr Monk. "Rules are rules. Don't let me see him again or your parents will hear about it."

Bertie tried to argue but Mr Monk was in no mood to listen. He dragged Whiffer towards the exit. At the gates, they found Nick and Flossy waiting for them.

Dirty Bertie

"Oh dear, Bertie!" Nick smirked. "Your pongy mutt's really *done it* this time. If only you'd trained him properly."

"Oh, put a sock in it, Nickerless," muttered Bertie.

"It's not fair!" Bertie complained as they walked home. "Surely he can't just ban Whiffer!"

"He probably can," said Darren. "He's in charge so he can do what he likes."

"But how does he know it was Whiffer?" asked Bertie. "Nobody actually *saw* him do it."

"Whiffer was the only dog around," Darren pointed out.

"Yes but I've seen Whiffer's poos a hundred times and they don't look like that," said Bertie.

Eugene looked thoughtful for a moment.

"I did see Nick sneaking off with Flossy while Mr Monk was yelling at you," he said. "He seemed in a big hurry."

Bertie stopped in his tracks.

"Why didn't you say so before?" he cried. "I knew it! That snooty poodle was the pooper. Wait till I tell Mr Monk!"

"It won't do any good," said Darren. "Mr Monk's already made up his mind. He's never liked you anyway."

This was true, thought Bertie, but he had to clear Whiffer's name somehow. The park was Whiffer's favourite place and where else could they go for walks? There was only one answer.

"We'll just have to prove Whiffer didn't do it," said Bertie.

"How can we do that?" asked Eugene.

"By catching whoever did," replied Bertie. "I bet you a million pounds it was Flossy."

"You might be right," said Eugene.
"But how are we going to prove it?"

"Tomorrow we're going back to stake
out the park," said Bertie. "We'll call it
Operation Whodunnit."

"Ha ha!" laughed Darren. "You mean
Operation *Poodunnit*!"

CHAPTER 3

The next day they returned to the park after school. It was the perfect chance to put *Operation Poodunnit* into action. Eugene had brought his binoculars while Bertie had brought Whiffer because his parents didn't yet know about the ban.

At the gates Bertie tied Whiffer's lead to the railings.

"It's not for long," he told him. "We'll get you back in the park, I promise."

Whiffer whined miserably as they walked off. Bertie had never left him outside the park before.

Along the path they ran into Mr Monk sweeping up leaves.

"Back again?" he grunted. "I hope you haven't brought that smelly mutt of yours?"

"I left him outside," replied Bertie. "And he's not smelly either, he had a bath last month."

They walked on till they were out of sight.

"So what's the master plan?" asked Darren.

"Simple, we hide and keep watch," said Bertie. "And when we catch Flossy in the act we make sure Mr Monk knows about it."

"If it *was* Flossy," said Eugene, but Bertie wasn't listening. He'd already crawled into the bushes.

They hid there for ages. One or two joggers ran by and the playground filled up. At long last a woman came along the path with a little pug. It sniffed around the bushes where they were hiding. Then its tail began to twitch.

"BONZO! Bonzo, *come on!*" shouted the woman.

Bonzo gave a bark and scurried after her.

"Rats!" sighed Darren. "Just when he was about to do a poo!"

Another half an hour went by. Dogs came and went – a Dalmatian, a bulldog, a sausage dog and four yappy puppies. But none of them stopped to do their business or even to wee against a tree. There was no sign of Flossy either.

"That's it, I give up!" groaned Darren. "This is a waste of time!"

"They'll be closing the park soon," yawned Eugene.

Bertie stood up and immediately

ducked back down again.

"It's Nick!" he hissed. "He's coming this way!"

This was it, their big chance to catch Flossy in the act. Bertie watched as Nick let Flossy off her lead. Flossy bounded off... Uh oh – she was coming straight towards the bushes. She sniffed around then began barking excitedly.

"SHOO!" hissed Bertie. "Go away, you dopey dog!"

Footsteps came closer. A grinning face peered down at them.

"Hello, Bertie!" said Nick. "What are you doing in there?"

CHAPTER 4

Bertie, Darren and Eugene crawled out
of the bushes. It looked like *Operation
Poodunnit* was a hopeless failure.

"Well?" said Nick. "What's going on?"

"Mind your own business," said Bertie.
"We were playing a game."

"Hide and seek," said Eugene.

Nick raised his eyebrows. "Really?

Dirty Bertie

Hide and seek with binoculars?"

"It's Extreme Hide and Seek, the rules are complicated," explained Bertie.

Nick snorted, not believing a word of it. He changed the subject.

"Isn't that your dog, Sniffer, sitting outside?" he asked.

"His name's Whiffer," said Bertie. "And he's not allowed in, as you know."

"Oh, yes, I forgot he's banned!" chortled Nick. "Flossy would hate to be left outside, but then she's so well trained she never gets into trouble."

Bertie scowled. "Whiffer's trained too."

"Oh yes?" sneered Nick. "What can he do – fetch a stick?"

"Loads of things," said Bertie. "He can beg for a start."

This was almost true. Whiffer begged by following Bertie all around the house until he got fed. It was the simple commands he hadn't mastered, like 'Sit' or 'Stay'. Flossy was so perfect she probably obeyed Nick's every order, thought Bertie. Wait a moment … he'd just had a brilliant idea! If he knew one thing about Nick it was that he loved to show off.

"Anyway, I bet Flossy doesn't *always* obey you," said Bertie.

"Of course she does, dumbo! I'll show you if you like," said Nick.

He turned to Flossy who was nosing in a pile of leaves.

"FLOSSY!" barked Nick, sounding like a sergeant major. "FLOSSY, SIT!"

Flossy immediately sat down.

"That's easy, any dog can do that," scoffed Bertie.

"Watch this then," said Nick. "FLOSSY! Roll over!"

Flossy rolled over in the leaves.

"Aww! That's so cute!" cooed Eugene.

"Nothing special," said Bertie. "Can she do any tricks?"

"Of course she can," boasted Nick. He brought out a tennis ball from his pocket and threw it high in the air. Flossy jumped and caught it neatly in her mouth. Nick bounced the ball and Flossy caught it a second time. Finally, he rolled the ball to her. Flossy trapped it under one paw, before batting it back.

Eugene clapped. Even Darren was impressed.

"You see?" crowed Nick triumphantly. "Like I said, she can do anything."

"Well, not *anything*," snorted Bertie.

"Anything I've taught her," insisted Nick.

"Okay, you told us she only poos when you tell her," said Bertie.

"It's true! She does!" beamed Nick.

"Well, I don't believe it," said Bertie, nudging Darren. "No dog is *that* well trained."

"Yeah, you're making it up," said Darren, catching on.

"I'm not!" said Nick indignantly. "I'll prove it if you like."

"Go on then, we're waiting," said Bertie.

He'd just caught sight of Mr Monk over Nick's shoulder. He was pushing his wheelbarrow down the path towards them. This was perfect timing. With any luck the head gardener would arrive right on cue.

"Flossy!" cried Nick, crouching down.

"Flossy, do-do time!"

Flossy looked up. For a moment Bertie thought she hadn't understood.

"DO-DO TIME, FLOSSY!" sang Nick. Flossy squatted down obediently. Her tail twitched and a neat little poop plopped on to the grass.

Nick clapped his hands with delight.

"See! I told you!" he whooped.

"OI! YOU!" roared a voice behind him. Mr Monk threw down his wheelbarrow and came marching towards them. All the colour drained from Nick's face. He tried to hide the evidence but it was too late.

"Can't you read the signs?" snarled Mr Monk. "No dog fouling in the park!"

"But it wasn't my fault! Bertie made her do it!" wailed Nick.

"Don't talk rubbish, she's your dog you should control her!" snapped Mr Monk. "She's banned. Now off you go!"

Nick gave Bertie a furious look. He knew he'd been tricked but there was nothing he could do about it. He slunk off towards the gates with Flossy trotting at his heels. Bertie turned to Mr Monk.

"You see? I told you the phantom pooper wasn't Whiffer!" he said. "It was Nick's poodle all the time."

Mr Monk shovelled the pile from the grass with a look of disgust.

"So is the ban lifted?" Bertie kept on. "Is Whiffer allowed back in the park?"

Mr Monk pulled a face. Given what he'd just witnessed, he didn't have much choice.

"Yes, I suppose so," he sighed.

Bertie gave a whoop of joy and ran off towards the gates. Wait till he told Whiffer!

Five minutes later Bertie and his friends watched Whiffer race across the park towards the trees.

"Look at him go!" laughed Bertie. "He loves this park."

"He does look happy to be back," agreed Darren.

"Wait, why's he stopped? What's he doing now?" asked Eugene.

Bertie grabbed Eugene's binoculars to take a closer look.

"OH NO!" he groaned.

TEACHER!

BEST
TEACHER
AWARD

CHAPTER 1

It was assembly and Bertie sat in the hall listening to Miss Skinner drone on.

"As you know we've had one or two problems with the heating, especially the radiators in Miss Boot's classroom," said the head teacher.

One or two problems? thought Bertie, it was like the Arctic in there! If this went on much longer he'd probably turn into an iceberg. He was already wearing his coat and hat, plus three pairs of woolly socks.

"Mr Grouch tells me he's called a plumber so I'm sure the problem will be fixed soon," said Miss Skinner. "But now some exciting news – I'm proud to tell you that one of our teachers has been shortlisted for Teacher of the Year."

A buzz of excitement went round the hall. Teacher of the Year? *Who on earth could it be?* thought Bertie. Maybe kind Miss Darling or weedy Mr Weakly who let them do whatever they liked?

Miss Skinner paused dramatically.

"So will you all join me in a big round of applause for … Miss Boot."

A gasp went up. Bertie thought he

might die of shock. Miss Boot? She had to be kidding! Darren and Eugene gaped at each other. Miss Boot came forward blushing modestly as everyone clapped.

"Thank you," she said. "It's obviously a great honour to be considered for this award. Perhaps my hard work, dedication and general excellence caught the judges' attention. I'd like to thank everyone who supported me."

As they filed out of the hall, Bertie still couldn't believe it.

"*Miss Boot?*" he said. "Are they out of their minds?"

"She has been teaching for a hundred years," said Eugene.

"I know," said Bertie. "But the award isn't for Oldest Teacher on the Planet."

"She does have some good points," Darren argued.

"Like what?" asked Bertie.

Darren tried to think. "Well, she's always nice to Snuffles."

"He's a hamster!" said Bertie. "She's never nice to me! How did they choose Miss Boot? What idiot would even suggest her?"

"Actually it was me," said a voice. They turned to see Know-All Nick,

smiling at them
smugly.

"*You?* You put
her up for this?"
cried Bertie.

"Of course! She's
my favourite teacher," said Nick.
"And not just because she always
gives me top marks."

"But how did you do it?" asked
Darren.

"Easy peasy," said Nick. "I wrote the
judges a letter. I said Miss Boot's the
best teacher in the universe. She's kind,
patient and she never has favourites."

"Apart from you," snorted Bertie.

"Anyway, it looks like my letter did
the trick," said Nick. "And Miss Boot's
promised me a gold star for writing it."

CHAPTER 2

Back in class everyone sat shivering in their coats and hats. It was all right for Miss Boot, thought Bertie, she had a big cape that made her look like Batman. For once she delayed getting straight down to work while she answered their questions about the award.

"Will you win, Miss?" asked Trevor.

"Of course she'll win, stupid," sighed Nick.

"Obviously that's not for me to decide," smiled Miss Boot. "But I hope they'll bear in mind my years of experience."

"Will you be famous?" asked Amanda. "Will you be on TV?"

Miss Boot laughed. "Let's not get too carried away," she said. "I'm on the shortlist but the judges decide who's in the final."

Bertie's hand shot up.

"Can anyone be a judge?" he asked.

"Of course not," snapped Miss Boot. "The judges are all experts in education. As a matter of fact one of them will be coming to watch me teach. We've no idea when, so I shall expect you *all* to be on your best behaviour."

Bertie wondered why Miss Boot was looking at him – he was always on his best behaviour!

"What's the prize if you win?" he asked. "Do you get a medal?"

"It's not the Olympics, Bertie," sighed Miss Boot. "Obviously what counts is the honour of winning Teacher of the Year. You never know where it might lead."

"Where?" asked Bertie, puzzled.

"Well, to a promotion for instance," said Miss Boot. Bertie hadn't a clue what she meant. He thought only football teams got promotion.

At break time Miss Boot was surrounded by a group of admiring children. She seemed to be enjoying the attention.

"If it was Worst Teacher of the Year
I could believe it," Bertie grumbled. "But
how can she be the best?"

"The others must be *really* terrible,"
said Darren.

"But there are loads of good
teachers," Eugene argued.

"Well I blame Know-All Nick," said
Bertie. "Making up all that stuff about
her being kind and fair. And what did

she mean about a promotion?"

"Maybe she wants to be a head teacher," Eugene suggested.

"But we've already got Miss Skinner," Darren pointed out.

"I know, but she could always become head at another school," said Eugene.

Bertie blinked. Why had he never thought of that before? All this time he'd lived in hope that Miss Boot would retire or move to Australia. Yet the answer to his prayers was staring him in the face.

"That's it," he cried. "If she became head at another school we'd be rid of her for good!"

No more spelling tests or piles of homework. This would be a dream come true. Their new teacher would probably hand out free ice cream every week!

"We have to make sure she wins," said Bertie.

Darren shrugged. "I don't see how."

"It's obvious," said Bertie. "When the judge comes we have to convince them that Nick was right: Miss Boot is the best teacher in the universe."

"But she's not," argued Eugene.

"*We* know that, but *they* don't," said Bertie. "We'll just go on and on about how clever, amazing and wonderful she is."

"You mean tell whopping great lies?" said Darren.

"Exactly," said Bertie.

It wouldn't be easy but it would be worth it in the end. Goodbye Miss Boot, hello freedom!

CHAPTER 3

The next day Bertie's classroom still felt like an ice-box. Miss Boot wore a fur hat and made them all do star jumps to keep warm. Bertie, Darren and Eugene were on red alert. All morning they kept an eye out for any visitor who might be a judge. Darren thought he'd spotted someone but it turned out to be

Trevor's mum dropping off his PE kit.

Finally after lunch they were returning to class when Bertie saw a visitor in reception.

"Look, that's her!" he whispered.

"Are you sure?" asked Darren.

"Of course!" said Bertie. "Look at her bag."

The woman wore denim dungarees and carried a large leather bag.

"She's a bit scruffy for a judge," said Eugene. "Wouldn't they be smarter?"

"That's her disguise," said Bertie. "I bet she doesn't want us to *suspect* she's a judge."

They caught up with the visitor as she headed down the corridor.

"Hello! Can we help you?" asked Bertie.

"Oh yes, I'm looking for Miss Boot's class," said the woman.

Bertie gave Darren and Eugene a meaningful look. This was their big chance to make sure Miss Boot won Teacher of the Year.

"We could show you round if you like," offered Bertie.

"Thank you, but I really should see Miss Boot," said the woman.

"We can take you, we're in her class," said Eugene.

Bertie led the way, though not in the right direction. He'd decided a grand tour of the school would make a good impression. After taking their visitor on a lap of the hall he stopped to point out a dusty cabinet.

"And these are all our trophies," he said. "That one was for the junior quiz, that's the football cup and that's for … um … water-skiing. Miss Boot teaches them all."

"Goodness, she sounds amazing!" said the visitor.

"She *is* amazing," said Darren. "If you ask me she should be Teacher of the Year."

They all nodded their heads in agreement.

"That's great but where's her class?

I thought you were taking me?" said the woman.

"Not far now," said Bertie, moving on. He stopped at a door and threw it open.

"These are the girls' toilets," he said. "Miss Boot built them herself."

"She *built* them?" repeated the woman.

Dirty Bertie

"Oh yes, with her own hands," said Bertie. "Take a look."

The visitor stepped inside. The moment she did, Bertie shut the door behind her and leaned against it.

"HEY!" cried the visitor.

"What are you doing?" asked Darren.

"Just keep her busy for a few minutes while I warn Miss Boot she's here," whispered Bertie.

Dirty Bertie

"How do we do that?" panicked Eugene.

"I don't know, show her the sick room," said Bertie.

He hurried off, ignoring the loud complaints coming from the toilets. He hoped Miss Boot would be grateful for helping her win. If anyone ought to get a medal it was him!

CHAPTER 4

Outside the head's office, Bertie almost bumped into Miss Skinner. She was talking to a man with a mop of grey hair.

"I'm afraid the heating's been a nightmare," she was saying. "It'll be such a relief to get it fixed…" Seeing Bertie, she broke off. "Ah Bertie, can you take Mr Marks to your class? He's here to see

Dirty Bertie

Miss Boot."

Bertie nodded. Another visitor! You waited ages then suddenly you got two at once. This one was obviously the plumber since Miss Skinner had been talking about the heating. About time too, thought Bertie, he was running out of socks.

"So you're in Miss Boot's class?" said the man, trying to keep up. "Would you say she's a good teacher?"

"Miss Boot? HUH!" laughed Bertie. "She's probably the worst teacher in the universe. Most of the time she never stops shouting."

The man looked shocked.

"But I thought she was in the running for a teaching award?" he said.

"She is," agreed Bertie. "But only because Know-All Nick wrote a pack of

Dirty Bertie

lies about her. We still want her to win though."

"You do?" said Mr Marks.

"Oh yes, that way we might get rid of her," said Bertie.

The man ran a hand through his grey hair. He went on asking questions about Miss Boot. Was she fair-minded? Patient? Inspiring? Bertie thought for a moment.

"I think 'scary' is a better word," he said. "Even the teachers are terrified of her."

He was surprised a plumber was so
interested – surely he should have been
asking about radiators!

Finally they reached the class and
Bertie hurried inside.

"Bertie! Where have you been? Get
to your seat immediately," barked Miss
Boot. "And where are Darren and
Eugene?"

"We've been busy looking after
visitors," explained Bertie. "Darren and
Eugene are bringing *the other one*." He
winked at her using both eyes.

"What?" said Miss Boot.

Bertie pointed to Mr Marks who was
standing in the doorway.

"This one's here about the heating,"
he explained.

"The heating! Why didn't you say so?"

cried Miss Boot.

Mr Marks smiled. "Oh yes, Miss Skinner was telling me about your radiators," he said. "I'm afraid I'm no expert. Ha ha!"

"You better be," snapped Miss Boot. "What took you so long?"

Mr Marks blinked. "I beg your pardon?"

"It's been two days," grumbled Miss Boot. "It's like a freezer in here so kindly stop dithering and get on with the job."

The visitor bristled. "Right, well, if you say so," he said huffily. "I'll be over here."

He sat down at an empty desk and took out a notebook and pen. Bertie frowned. Surely a plumber's bag would be full of spanners and stuff? Unless… A worrying thought crossed his mind – had Miss Skinner actually *said* the man was a plumber?

Dirty Bertie

Miss Boot stood over him. "WHAT ON EARTH ARE YOU PLAYING AT?" she boomed.

"Me? I'm … um … just observing," spluttered the visitor.

"We're not paying you to *observe*," thundered Miss Boot. "You're here to fix the radiators!"

"But…"

Just then the door flew open. Eugene and Darren burst in with the other visitor.

"Now what?" groaned Miss Boot. "Who in heaven's name is this?"

"I'm so sorry, Miss Boot, I got held up," said the woman. "I'm Clare from Bathgate Plumbers."

UH OH! Bertie slid down lower in his seat. Miss Boot looked from one visitor to the other.

"But if *you're* the plumber, then who is this?" she croaked.

Bertie was pretty sure he could guess. The man with grey hair rose stiffly to his feet.

"Mr Marks, from the Teaching Awards," he said. "I believe you were told I'd be paying you a visit, Miss Boot?"

Dirty Bertie

Miss Boot's mouth opened but no sound came out. She looked as if she wanted to crawl into a hole. How could this have happened? There was only one explanation.

"BERTIE!" she bellowed.

"I was only trying to help!" wailed Bertie. "How was I to know?"

Miss Boot tried to apologize but it was too late. Mr Marks had seen quite enough. In fact he said the letter they'd received about Miss Boot appeared to be a pack of lies.

Once he was gone, Miss Boot closed the door. She stood for a moment breathing hard and counting to ten. The finals, the awards, all her hopes of glory had gone up in smoke thanks to one person.

Dirty Bertie

Bertie raised his hand.

"Does this mean you won't be Teacher of the Year?"

Miss Boot gritted her teeth. "That now looks highly unlikely," she said.

"So you won't be leaving to become a head teacher somewhere else?" asked Bertie.

Miss Boot smiled thinly and folded her arms.

"No Bertie, don't worry," she said. "I shall be here teaching you for many, many years to come."

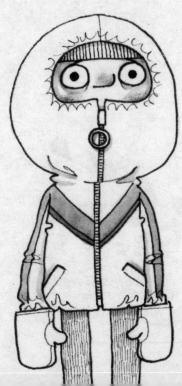

EXTRAS!

BRAD SPLIT
SCENE 17   TAKE 1
"EXTRAS"
"APPOINTMENT WITH DANGER"

CHAPTER 1

Bertie was having breakfast with his
family. He splashed milk into his cereal
bowl while Dad read a letter that had
just arrived in the post.

"I don't believe it!" Dad burst out.
"I've got a part!"

"A part of what?" asked Bertie.

"A part *in a film*!" said Dad.

"What? How? When?" asked Bertie, Mum and Suzy, all talking at once.

"Remember I signed up with that company that hires extras?" said Dad. "Well they want me to come to the film studios on Saturday."

"What's an extra?" Bertie asked.

"It's someone who plays a small part in a film," explained Mum.

"I'd love to be *anything* in a film," said Suzy.

"Me too!" said Bertie.

He'd watched millions of films but no one told him you could actually *be* in one! But why would a film company want his dad of all people?

"How come they chose you? You're not even an actor," he pointed out.

"I am!" said Dad huffily. "I've been in

lots of plays. They may only be amateur but it's still acting."

Bertie had seen these plays — mostly his dad just stood around dressed as a policeman. Bertie, on the other hand, had played a dog in *Oliver*, which involved a lot of barking.

"Anyway, extras don't really have to act," said Dad.

"What do they do then?" asked Bertie.

"They're just there in the background," said Dad. "If there's a crowd or an army, those parts will be played by extras."

"Brilliant!" said Bertie. He'd be good in an army, perhaps as a Viking raider or a pirate captain. He had a sword and an eye patch already.

"What's the film called?" asked Suzy.

"*Appointment with Danger*, starring Brad Split," said Dad.

"Ooh, Brad Split, he's amazing," said Mum. "And *so* handsome!"

"UGH! MU-UM!" groaned Suzy.

"But can anybody be an extra?" Bertie wanted to know.

"No," said Dad quickly. "And before you ask, you're too young."

Dirty Bertie

"I could look a lot older if I wore Gran's glasses," suggested Bertie.

"Don't get any ideas," said Dad. "I'm the one they invited to be an extra. They didn't say 'Bring your whole family'."

Bertie sighed. It wasn't fair, why should his dad be the only one in a film? He'd be great as an extra and who

knew where it might lead. Imagine if he became a famous movie star! They'd have to move to Hollywood. He'd need a gigantic, open-top car so he could wave to all his fans.

"Couldn't I come and watch?" he pleaded.

"Definitely not," said Dad.

"PLEEEASE!" begged Bertie. "I won't get in the way. I've always wanted to see how films are made."

"I suppose it could be educational," suggested Mum.

"You can't be serious! It's a terrible idea!" said Dad.

"But Mum's coming to my dance show on Saturday," Suzy reminded them.

"Oh yes, I'm not taking Bertie to *that*," said Mum.

"Fine, I'd rather go with Dad," said Bertie.

Dad raised his eyes to the heavens.

Dirty Bertie

Why did this always happen to him?

"Okay," he sighed. "I'll take him!"

"YAHOOOO!" yelled Bertie. A film studio! This was going to be the best day of his life!

CHAPTER 2

On Saturday morning they arrived promptly at Pinecone Studios.

"Remember you're just here to watch, leave the talking to me," warned Dad.

Bertie was hoping to catch sight of Brad Split but there was no sign of him in the car park.

At reception they were met by Cleo,

one of the assistant directors. She
checked Dad's name on her list.

"Ah yes, you're in Red Group," she
said. Her eyes fell on Bertie.

"I'm so sorry, I had to bring my son
along," Dad explained. "This is Bertie,
but he's only here to watch."

Cleo looked doubtful. "I'll have to
check with Joel, he's the director," she
said. "We don't usually allow children
on set."

"I won't get in the way," promised
Bertie. "Is the film about monsters or
aliens?"

"Neither. It's a spy film set in the
Second World War," replied Cleo.

Even better, thought Bertie. He'd make
a brilliant spy – he was great at sneaking
biscuits from the kitchen cupboard. He

stood on tiptoe to look taller.

"I was wondering, do you need any more extras?" he asked hopefully.

"I'm afraid not," said Cleo.

Dad glared at him. Just then a man appeared wearing a back-to-front baseball cap.

"This is Joel, our director," said Cleo. "I was just explaining we don't really allow children on set."

Joel grinned at Bertie. "First time at a film studio?" he asked.

"Yes, it is," said Bertie excitedly. "My dad's an extra."

"Awesome! We can't make the film without extras," said Joel.

"*I'd* make a great extra," said Bertie enthusiastically. "I'm good at standing in the background."

Joel laughed. "I like your style, buddy," he said. "How are the numbers looking today, Cleo?"

Cleo checked her list.

"We're one short in Red Group," she said. "Someone just called in sick."

Bertie's heart leaped. Surely if someone was sick they would need an *extra* extra? And luckily he was right here and available!

"What about me?" he asked.

Joel thought for a moment. "Sure, why not?" he said. "It might be good to have another kid in the street scenes."

"YAHOOO!" cried Bertie.

"Are you sure that's a good idea?" asked Dad. "He's never been in a film."

"It'll be fine, as long as he does what he's told," said Joel. "You can do that, can't you, buddy?"

"Of course," said Bertie. He had to do what he was told at school and sometimes he even managed it.

Cleo wrote his name on her list. "Right, Bertie," she said. "I suppose we'll have to find you a costume. Follow me."

Bertie could hardly believe his luck. *Me in an actual film!* he thought. *Wait till Darren and Eugene hear about this!*

CHAPTER 3

Half an hour later they emerged from the costume department. Bertie's costume was a big disappointment. It consisted of an itchy jumper, baggy shorts and a cap. Apparently this was how children dressed in wartime. Dad meanwhile wore a raincoat and hat.

Bertie expected to be thrown straight

into the action with car chases and explosions. Instead they were shown to a dingy room where other extras were reading or staring at their phones. There was one upside to this – the food, there was loads of it and it was all free!

Bertie loaded up his plate with crisps, doughnuts, buns and a chocolate Chunky bar. He could always go back for more later.

"You're not really going to eat all that?" said Dad, looking up from his book.

"I *am*," said Bertie. "I hardly had any breakfast."

"For goodness' sake don't make yourself sick," sighed Dad.

Bertie had only taken one bite when a man stuck his head round the door.

"Red group, you're up!" he said.

Dirty Bertie

"Follow me, please."

Dad jumped up. "Heavens! That's us!"

"But I haven't finished eating!" protested Bertie.

"You'll just have to leave it," said Dad.

Bertie stared. He couldn't leave all that free food! Who knew when he'd get another chance to eat? Stuffing his pockets with doughnuts and the chocolate bar, he hurried after Dad.

Soon after they arrived on the film set with the rest of Red Group. Bertie stared in boggle-eyed wonder. In front of them was an entire street complete with dirty brick houses and old, bubble-shaped cars. There were lights everywhere and the camera crew buzzed around getting ready.

"Wowee!" gasped Bertie.

"Impressive, isn't it?" said Dad. "Now remember what they said – don't talk to the actors, never look at the camera and most of all…"

"Do what you're told!" repeated Bertie. Honestly, it was like being back at school!

Dirty Bertie

Cleo explained the scene they were going to film. Brad Split was about to meet his co-star, Anna, who was playing a beautiful spy. As extras their role was simply to make the street look busy.

"Just walk by as if you're going somewhere," Cleo told them.

They waited while Joel explained something to Brad and Anna. Bertie tucked into a jammy doughnut.

Dad rolled his eyes. "Where did you get that?"

"From my pocket," said Bertie, licking his lips. "I'm still hungry!"

Just then Cleo called Red Group together to run through the scene.

"Bertie, can you hold your dad's hand?" she suggested.

Bertie frowned.

"It's acting,"
muttered Dad. "Just
do it."

After a few practice
runs they were ready
to shoot the scene.

A man held up a clapperboard.
"Quiet on set!" he cried. "Scene 17,
Take One. Action!"

They did the scene. In Bertie's view it
went perfectly. He held his dad's hand
and remembered not to smile or pull
faces at the camera. Unfortunately the
sound wasn't right so they had to do it
again. And again … and again.

"Why's it taking so long?" grumbled
Bertie. "Didn't they learn their lines?"

"Filming takes time, you just have to
be patient," replied Dad. Bertie decided

he might as well start on his chocolate bar, but Cleo was calling them back into position.

"Scene 17, Take 10. Action!" said the clapperboard man.

Bertie and Dad walked down the street for the umpteenth time.

"CUT!" cried Joel. "That worked for me. I think we finally got it."

Joel and Cleo watched the scene back on a screen.

"Wait, what's that?" asked Joel, pointing. "The kid's got something in his hand."

All eyes turned on Bertie. Reluctantly he brought out the Chunky bar he was hiding behind his back.

"It's only chocolate," he said. "I didn't get any lunch."

"You can see it in the shot!" moaned Joel. "Kids in wartime didn't have Chunky bars! They weren't even invented! You know what this means?"

"I'll have to eat an apple?" said Bertie.

"NO! It means we have to shoot the whole scene again *because of you!*" snapped Joel.

Dad made a big apology to everyone. Bertie couldn't see what all the fuss was about. Why leave free chocolate lying around if you weren't allowed to eat it?

CHAPTER 4

Filming went on into the afternoon. Red Group spent most of it sitting around in the dingy room. Dad finished his book while Bertie built a tower out of biscuits. Finally they were called back. Cleo explained that the next scene was a big one. Anna was trapped in a burning hotel and Brad would risk his life to rescue her.

Bertie waited as Red Group were handed their roles. Some were fetching buckets of water, while others played survivors of the fire. Bertie hoped he could help the fire brigade but Cleo had other ideas.

"We need someone to carry a ladder," she said.

Dad raised his hand. "I can do that."

"It'll be easier with two of us," said Bertie.

"I wouldn't bet on it," muttered Dad.

"It's simple. Just carry it across, from right to left," explained Cleo. "Don't take long because Brad needs a clear run to the hotel, understand?"

"Got it," said Dad.

"Copy that," said Bertie.

This was more like it, he thought,

playing a ladder carrier was an important part. They'd be close to the action and to Brad, the star of the film. With a bit of luck they might even get their faces on screen.

They took up their starting positions. Brad got ready to roar in on his motorbike. Bertie held the front of the ladder with Dad bringing up the rear.

"You know what to do?" asked Dad.

Bertie nodded. "Just carry the ladder."

"Yes from right to left," said Dad. "And quickly so we're out of the way."

"I've got it," said Bertie, although which way was right to left? He sometimes got the two mixed up.

"Scene 35, Take 1, Action!" cried the clapperboard man.

Thick smoke rolled in and extras ran

in every direction. Sirens blared as fire
hoses aimed great jets of water at the
blazing hotel.

"GO!" cried Dad.

Bertie set off running, with the ladder
banging against his legs. He dodged a
line of people passing buckets of water.
Where now? With all the smoke he
couldn't see a thing!

"Keep going! Right to left!" hissed Dad.

Right to left – which way was that?
Bertie tried to remember. Left was the
other way, he decided swinging round.

"*NO, THAT WAY!*" cried Dad. A tug
of war broke out with the ladder in the
middle. Bertie heard a motorbike screech
to a halt. Brad Split jumped off and came
running straight towards them.

"MOVE!" yelled the film star.

Dirty Bertie

Bertie tried to move but Dad was pulling the ladder the other way. Brad kept going. At the last moment he launched himself into the air, trying to hurdle the ladder. He would have made it too, if his foot hadn't caught on the top. Bertie watched as he flew through the air like Superman. Luckily he landed on top of one of the fire fighters. They both hit the ground, face down in a puddle.

"AND CUT!" yelled Joel.

Oops! thought Bertie, that hadn't exactly gone to plan. Brad sat up, wiping mud from his face. Dad buried his head in his hands. This was it, thought Bertie, the end of their film career. They'd probably be sent home in disgrace.

Joel helped Brad to his feet.

"Brad baby, that was *awesome!*" he chuckled. "And listen, it's given me a great idea. Let's shoot it again, only this time you grab the ladder from the kid. You climb up through the smoke, rescue Anna and carry her down in your arms. It'll be *spectacular!*"

Bertie blinked. *The kid?* That was him! Maybe they wouldn't be sent home after all? Better still, it sounded like he'd landed a bigger part in the film!

Dirty Bertie

Dad came over looking mystified.

"How do you do it?" he asked.

Bertie shrugged. "Don't ask me, I'm just doing what I'm told."

He might even get his name in the credits: *Boy with ladder – Bertie Burns*. After all, even film stars had to start somewhere!